Full name:	Rupert Alexander Grint	Full name:	Emma Charlotte Duerre Watson
Nickname:	Rupe	Nickname:	Em
Harry Potter character:	Ron Weasley	*Harry Potter* character:	Hermione Granger
Birthday:	August 24, 1988	Birthday:	April 15, 1990
Astro sign:	Virgo	Astro sign:	Aries

Full name:	Thomas Andrew Felton	Full name:	Daniel Jacob Radcliffe
Nickname:	Tom	Nickname:	Dan (not Danny!)
Harry Potter character:	Draco Malfoy	*Harry Potter* character:	Harry Potter
Birthday:	September 22, 1987	Birthday:	July 23, 1989
Astro sign:	Virgo	Astro sign:	Cancer/Leo — It's on the cusp.

Harry Potter
AND THE GOBLET OF FIRE™

COLORING
BOOK

SCHOLASTIC INC.

New York   Toronto   London   Auckland   Sydney
Mexico City   New Delhi   Hong Kong   Buenos Aires

ISBN 0-439-63295-1

12 11 10 9 8 7 6 5 4 3 2 1   5 6 7 8 9/0

Designed by Two Red Shoes Design
Printed in the U.S.A.

First printing, November 2005

Collect all of the
Harry Potter and the Goblet of Fire books.

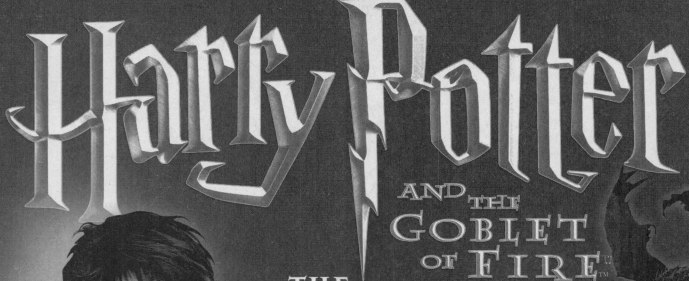

AND THE GOBLET OF FIRE™

THE HOTTEST
MOVIE OF THE YEAR

www.scholastic.com
www.harrypotter.com

SCHOLASTIC